THE LEGEND OF DAVE THE VILLAGER 5

by Dave Villager

First Print Edition (August 2019)

BOOK FIVE:
Invasion

The Legend of Dave the Villager 5

CHAPTER ONE
Land Ahoy!

"Land ahoy!" Porkins shouted. "I say, chaps, I can see land!"

Dave and Carl ran out from their cabins to look. Dave was wearing his huge iron golem suit.

Porkins was right, Dave was pleased to see—there were lush green hills in the distance and a golden beach. It was the first land they'd seen since leaving Cool Island three days earlier.

"At last," said Carl. "I've had enough of the ocean to last me a lifetime."

"Does it look like an island?" Dave asked Porkins, coming over to join him at the ship's controls.

"I don't think so," said Porkins. "I think we're finally back to the mainland."

Dave breathed a sigh of relief. Like Carl, he was fed up of being at sea. He wanted to get back to solid ground and resume his journey to find an ender portal.

It wasn't long before they reached the beach. Porkins dropped the anchor, then they swam to the shore.

"Land!" said Carl happily, rolling in the sand in his iron golem armor.

"Are you going to throw an ender eye?" Porkins asked Dave. "To see which way we should go?"

"I'll wait until we're a bit further inland," said Dave. "I don't want to waste them more than I have to."

So Dave, Porkins and Carl made their way across the beach, walking towards the green hills and trees that lay beyond.

"I say, what about the ship?" said Porkins, looking back at the ocean. Their small ship, the one the people of Cool Island had given them, was bobbing on the waves.

"Leave it," said Carl. "We don't need it anymore."

"I guess not," said Porkins.

They soon found themselves walking across a large plains biome. Sheep and rabbits were grazing on the grass and there were flowers everywhere. Porkins kept stopping to pick them.

"What do you need flowers for?" Carl asked. "Flowers are stupid."

"Flowers are good for dyes," said Porkins.

Carl rolled his eyes. "We're meant to be going to kill a dragon, not making pretty dresses."

"I always fancied some pink leather armor," said Porkins. "I think it would look rather fetching."

"You're pink already!" said Carl, in disbelief.

"Come on Carl, let Porkins pick flowers in peace," said Dave. "Talking of armor, we got so much diamond from Cool City that we ought to build some. Weapons too. You sure you wouldn't rather have new diamond armor, Porkins? It's stronger than leather, according to my crafting book."

"I guess so," said Porkins. "But I'll make myself some pink leather armor as well. For special occasions."

They soon came across some cows. Carl used his new iron golem strength to slay them, then Dave cooked the raw beef into steak and Porkins took the leather to make his armor. By the time Dave had finished cooking, Porkins was dressed head to toe in pink armor.

"Pretty snazzy, huh chaps?" said Porkins.

"You look like a giant sausage," said Carl.

They sat down and ate, then, because the sun was starting to go down, Dave made them a small house with three beds.

"Goodnight chaps," said Porkins, as they snuggled down into their beds.

"Goodnight, Porkins," said Dave.

For the first time in a long time, Dave was starting to

feel good about their adventure. For too long they'd been distracted from their main quest, caught up in other adventures. But now, finally, they were on their way. All they had to do was keep on following the eyes of ender, and soon they'd find another stronghold. Then they could go to the End and slay the ender dragon, and Dave would be the hero he'd always dreamed of being.

Dave also began to wonder how Steve was getting on. Steve had been on a quest to slay the ender dragon as well, but Dave knew that Steve was easily distracted. Hopefully Steve had found something else to interest him, and had forgotten all about it. Dave's relationship with Steve was complicated: he'd started out hating him, but now... now he wasn't so sure.

Finally, Dave drifted off to sleep.

The next morning, Dave, Porkins and Carl destroyed the little house, putting the tiny blocks back in Dave's rucksack.

"Right," said Dave, "let's see what direction we need to go."

He took out an eye of ender and threw it into the sky. For a moment it hovered in place, then it zoomed off into the distance.

"This way then," said Dave, then he, Porkins and Carl followed the path the eye had taken.

They had only been walking an hour or so when they

started to hear sounds coming from up ahead.

"What is that?" said Porkins. "I recognize the sound, but I can't ruddy well put my finger on it."

"It sounds like... digging," said Dave. "But I don't think it's just one person digging. I think it's lots."

They kept walking. As they got nearer it was clear that Dave was right: it was digging. But it sounded like *hundreds* of people digging.

Eventually they came over a hill and finally caught sight of the diggers. In front of them was a huge pit, as big as a small town, and hundreds of diggers were using pickaxes to chip away at it. As they got closer, Dave saw the pit already went down to bedrock: the diggers were just making it wider.

"They must be mining for emerald or gold," said Carl. "Maybe there's a mining town nearby."

"Shall we go and introduce ourselves?" Porkins asked Dave. "Maybe we can do some trading with them."

But something didn't seem right to Dave. On the face of it, it just looked like a normal mine, but there was something wrong.

Suddenly he realized what it was. Not all of the figures in the mine were villagers; some were pigmen. *Zombie* pigmen. And they weren't mining, they were guarding the villagers.

"Look," he whispered to Carl and Porkins, pointing at

the pigmen.

"Zombie pigmen!" exclaimed Porkins. "But what are they doing outside of the Nether?"

"I don't know and I don't want to know," said Carl. "Come on, let's take another route."

"No," said Dave, "we can't just leave those villagers. It looks they're being forced to mine against their will."

"I thought you wanted to find this stupid dragon and be a hero?" said Carl.

"I do," said Dave, "but part of being a hero is helping people in need. And those villagers need our help."

CHAPTER TWO

The Mine

By Dave's count, there were twenty zombie pigmen and over one-hundred villagers. The zombie pigmen were armed though, with gold swords.

"This will be an easy fight," said Carl. "Zombies are just mindless idiots. We'll just go in and bish, bash, bosh! They'll be defeated in no time."

"Those *mindless idiots* used to be my people," said Porkins sadly.

"Oh... Sorry Porkins," said Carl.

"But you're right though, old bean," said Porkins. "They're nothing but zombies now. I wish that wasn't the case, but it is. And we must defeat them to save those villager chaps."

"Ok," said Dave, "Porkins, you use your bow to take out the ones furthest away—the six down near the bottom of the pit. Carl, you quickly charge around and take out the eight at the top of the pit, and I'll take out the last six.

They're all gathered together around the middle of the pit, so I should be able to dispose of them quickly. We'll all attack together, to take them by surprise, so get in position and wait for my signal."

"What's the signal?" asked Carl.

"Um, I'll yell 'Now!'"

"Fair enough," said Carl.

"You sure you don't want some better armor?" Dave asked Porkins.

"Actually I think leather armor is better for my archery," said Porkins, "I can move easier in it than I can in diamond."

"Fair enough," said Dave.

Dave, Porkins and Carl all sneaked around the pit, getting into position. When Dave saw they were all ready, he took a deep breath, then yelled: "NOW!"

Porkins fired arrows at the zombie pigmen at the bottom of the pit, slaying them before they had a chance to realize what was happening. Carl used his huge iron arms to send the zombie pigmen around the top of the pit flying. Dave ran forward and slashed at the remaining pigmen. Once he'd attacked one, the rest came running at him, and he soon defeated them all.

The battle was over so quickly that the mining villagers were confused.

"What happened?" one asked.

"We saved your butts," said Carl, chambering down the pit to join Dave and Porkins.

"It's a creeper!" one of the villagers yelled. "A creeper... in an iron golem suit?!"

"Relax," said Dave, "he's a friend. We all are. We came to rescue you."

"Thanks," said a female villager in a white coat. "I'm Sally, by the way."

"Nice to meet you, Sally," said Dave. "What was going on here? Why were the pigmen making you mine?"

"*Zombie* pigmen," said Porkins. "Those chaps weren't pigmen anymore."

"Sorry Porkins," said Dave, "Good point."

"Where have you been?" Sally asked Dave. "I thought all villagers were being forced to dig these mines. When the pigmen invaded, we sent messages from village to village, and they'd all been invaded too."

"Invaded by pigmen?" asked Dave. "What's going on?"

Sally sighed. "I don't know where you've been, but a week ago nether portals started popping up in every village and town. I even heard reports that one appeared as far away as Villagertropolis. Zombie pigmen poured out of the portals and took over. Now they're forcing us to dig holes; they're looking for something called a *stronghold*.

Apparently they're these really old structures that the Old People built underground."

Dave's blood went cold. Herobrine had been looking for a stronghold. Could this be anything to do with him?

"Wait a minute," said Carl, "this doesn't make sense. How could the zombie pigmen give you orders? They can't even speak!"

"The pigmen are not alone," said Sally. "They seem to be controlled by witches. From what I've heard, there's one witch in every village, controlling the pigmen. Ours is called Dotty. She gives us the orders, and the pigmen make sure we do what we're told."

"Dotty!" said Porkins. "That's the dastardly witch who gave us the sleeping potion in our food. The one who brought us to Herobrine."

"You've seen Emperor Herobrine?" said Sally, sounding amazed. "I thought he was just a myth that the witches made up to keep us under control."

"Wait, why did you call him *Emperor* Herobrine?" asked Dave.

"Because that's what the witches call him," said Sally. "They say that he's their boss. That he's now the ruler of the world, and we have to do what he says."

"We go away for a week and the world gets taken over by Herobrine," said Carl. "Can't people take care of themselves?"

"Wait," said another villager. "A villager, a pigman and a creeper... you're not Dave, are you?"

"I am," said Dave.

"Oh dear," said the villager. "That's another thing that Herobrine is making us do: as well as digging for strongholds, we've been told to be on the lookout for a villager named Dave, who hangs out with a tiny creeper and a pigman."

"Do I look tiny to you?" asked Carl, flexing his iron muscles.

"And what are you meant to do if you find me?" asked Dave.

"Capture you," said the villager. "I don't know what you've done, Dave, but apparently Emperor Herobrine wants you alive."

"And are you going to bring me to him?" Dave asked.

The villager looked at Carl, then at Dave and Porkins with their weapons.

"Of course not," he said, smiling. But there was something about that smile that Dave didn't trust.

"What Adam is trying to say," said Sally, "is that we're very grateful to you for saving us."

Adam scoffed. "They haven't really saved us. There are still hundreds of pigmen back at the village."

"We can defeat those cads as well," said Porkins. "Dave, Carl and I are mighty warriors. We won the Cool Dude Battle Royale!"

"Never heard of it," said Adam. "Thanks for your help, but you should go. We'll have enough explaining to do when we return to the village without our zombie pigmen guards. If you come with us, there'll be no end of trouble."

"Adam," said Sally, "these three are warriors—they could help us! Even Emperor Herobrine is scared of Dave. They could help us defeat him and his pigmen once and for all."

"Are you mad?" said Adam. "Herobrine has taken over every village and town in the area. For all we know, he might have conquered the entire world. What use are these three going to be?"

"We've defeated Herobrine once and we can ruddy well do it again," said Porkins.

Porkins was stretching the truth a bit, Dave thought to himself. They hadn't really defeated Herobrine the last time they met, they'd merely escaped from him.

"Will you help us then?" Sally asked Dave. "Will you help us take back our village?"

Dave looked round. Some of the villagers looked as excited as Sally, but others looked worried, and some, like Adam, looked annoyed.

They're scared that I'll let them down, thought Dave.

15

It was all very well marching into a village and defeating a load of zombie pigmen, but if Herobrine's army was as big as it sounded, it would only be a temporary measure. Soon Herobrine would send more troops, and take the village back again.

"Can you sneak us into your village?" Dave asked. "If we can have a look round, maybe we can figure out a plan."

"Great!" said Sally excitedly.

Adam gave Carl and Porkins a disapproving look. "And how do you intend to sneak them in?" he said. "A creeper and a pig?"

"I'm a pig*man*, thank you," said Porkins.

"Do you have iron golems in your village?" Dave asked. "If we painted Carl's face gray, he could pretend to be one of them."

"I'm afraid we don't," said Sally. "The pigmen slew them all when they took over."

"Well, at least Porkins can pretend to be a zombie pigman," said Dave.

"What what what?" said Porkins, a look of shock on his face.

"All we have to do is put a bit of gray dye on your face in the right places," said Dave. "Maybe a bit of green too."

"Good job you picked all those flowers," grinned Carl.

"How can we hide Carl?" Dave asked Sally.

Sally took a long hard look at Carl.

"Well, you'll have to take off the iron golem armor," she said. "There's no way we can sneak you in in that thing."

"No way!" said Carl. "I'm not losing my iron golem suit."

"We can hide it somewhere near the village," Dave reassured him. "You can get it back later, Carl."

"Hmmph," said Carl.

"I've got it!" said Sally excitedly. "We can disguise you as a pig!"

"What?" said Carl. Now it was his turn to look shocked.

"Our village is full of pigs," said Sally, "we've been pig farmers for generations. No-one will look twice at you if you're covered in pink dye with an apple for a nose."

Porkins chuckled. "I say Carl, I think you'd look rather cute."

"Shut your mouth," said Carl. He didn't look very happy.

"Then that's settled then," said Dave. Porkins will disguise himself as a zombie pigman, Carl will disguise himself as a pig, and we'll go undercover in your village to see what's going on. But who should I say I am?"

"I'll tell everyone you're my long-lost cousin," said

Sally. "Although we'd better not call you Dave, as everyone is looking for a Dave. How about... Ian?"

"Ok, Ian it is," said Dave.

CHAPTER THREE
Greenleaf

Dave, Porkins, Carl and the villagers all began their long
trek back to the village.

"Our village is called Greenleaf," Sally told Dave as
they walked. "We're only a small community, but we're
proud pig farmers. We sell most of our pigs to
Villagertropolis and the big towns. Or at least we did,
before the zombie pigmen came. Now everyone is forced to
work in the pits."

"Pits?" said Dave. "There are more than one?"

"Yes," said Sally. "There are four in total. Dotty the
witch told us where to dig them. Apparently all the other
settlements taken over by the pigmen are digging pits as
well."

Herobrine really is desperate to find a stronghold,
Dave thought to himself. *But why?* The only theory he'd
come up with so far was that Herobrine must want to tame
the ender dragon, to use it for his evil deeds. But that

seemed too simple. From what Dave had seen of Herobrine, he was powerful enough already, without a dragon.

They came through some trees and finally they could see Greenleaf. It was only a small village, as Sally had said, and it was on the top of a small hill.

"Right," said Sally. "Porkins, Carl, you two ought to get in disguise."

Adam marched over.

"I've been talking with some of the others," he said, "and we've agreed that this is a stupid idea. Dave and his friends will get found out, and then we'll all be in trouble. Nothing good can come of this, mark my words."

"Do you really want to be digging mines for the rest of your life?" Sally asked him. "This could be our chance to fight back."

Adam said nothing, but he muttered something angrily under his breath.

"Attention everyone!" Sally said, talking to the rest of the villagers. "As you know, Dave and his friends are going to enter the village in secret, so please don't accidentally give them away. And don't tell anyone else about this either—we want to keep Dave's presence here as secret as possible for now, to stop the zombie pigmen from finding out."

"It's not the zombie pigmen I'm worried about," said

Adam. "They just do as they're told. It's Dotty we need to watch. If she suspects anything, she'll contact her boss. And then we'll have Herobrine to deal with."

"Well, let's make sure that doesn't happen," said Sally. She turned to Carl and Porkins. "Right you two, let's get you in disguise."

"Oh crumbs," said Porkins.

"Oh dear," said Carl.

"Oh, stop complaining," said Dave, grinning. "I'm sure you'll both look lovely."

Sally and a few of the villagers got to work on Porkins and Carl, using Porkins's flowers to make the appropriate dyes for their skin. It took all Dave's willpower not to burst out laughing.

When they were finished, it was quite a sight to behold. Porkins looked just like a real zombie pigman, with the makeup making it look like he had rotten flesh and exposed bone.

"I bet I look frightfully ugly," sighed Porkins.

"Um, no... you look... fine," said Dave.

But when the villagers finished applying Carl's makeup, Dave couldn't stop himself from laughing.

"Yeah, yeah, laugh it up," said Carl, unhappily.

"I'm sorry," said Dave, wiping tears of laughter from his eyes. "It's just you look so... so... so much like a pig."

The villagers had done a great job. All of Carl's skin was covered in pink dye, he had bits of bacon for ears and an apple for his nose, all tied on with string. The apple had been smothered with pink dye, with two black spots on it to look like nostrils.

"You'll fit right in with all our little piggies," said Sally, trying to be nice. "You look very cute."

"Bah!" said Carl.

"I say, Dave," said Porkins, "I've just realized—Dotty knows who you are. You'll need a disguise too."

"Oh dear," said Dave, "I never thought about that."

"Here," said Carl, "let me help."

He dipped his hand into some red dye, then wiped over the lower half of Dave's face.

"There you go," said Carl, "a lovely red beard."

"Uh, thanks," said Dave.

When everyone was ready, they continued the journey back to the village. The village was made up of small wooden houses; it reminded Dave of his own village, before Steve had blown it up with TNT, and it made him a bit homesick.

As they reached the first of the wooden buildings, two zombie pigmen came to meet them.

"Rrurk rrurk!" said one of the pigmen.

"Rrurk roik!" said the other.

"Hello," Sally said cheerily. "We're back for the day. No sign of a stronghold yet, I'm afraid."

"Can they understand what you're saying?" Dave whispered.

"I don't think so," Sally whispered. "Though they're not quite as dumb as they look. I think they know something's wrong."

They was a swishing sound, then a witch swooped down on elytra wings and landed in front of them.

It was Dotty.

"What happened to your pigman guards?" she asked Sally. "And who is this?" she said, looking at Dave.

"There was an ambush," said Sally. "A bunch of skeletons attacked us. The pigmen bravely stepped in to save us, but all of them were killed except one." She turned to Porkins.

"Um, rurk rurk!" said Porkins, doing his best zombie pigman impression.

Dotty gave him a suspicious look. Then she turned to Dave.

"Who are you, villager?" she asked.

"This is my cousin, D—Ian," said Sally.

"De-Ian?" said Dotty.

"Yes," said Sally, "De-Ian... Dean. His name is Dean."

"Ok," said Dotty. "Tell me, Dean, where do you come

from? And to what do we owe the pleasure of your company?"

"I'm... a humble pig farmer from the mountains, Dave said, trying to remember the fake story that Sally had made up for him. "But all my pigs were eaten by zombies, so I decided to come and live in Greenleaf, with my cousin, as I knew that they farm pigs here too." He turned to Carl. "This is the last pig I have left. The only one that survived."

"Oink oink," said Carl.

"Well if you're going to stay here, you'd better be prepared to dig," said Dotty. "Emperor Herobrine doesn't want any slackers in his empire. You work hard, you get to live."

"That's very generous," said Dave.

Dotty gave him a suspicious look, trying to work out if he was being rude or not.

"Just watch yourself, Dean," she said. "And remember, I'm in charge around here."

And with that, Dotty walked off. Dave watched her head into a building made of dark reddish brown bricks.

Nether brick, Dave realized. The nether brick building was the only building in the village not made of wood.

"That's where the nether portal is," Sally whispered. "Once the pigmen took over the village they built that building around the portal. The witch lives in there, and it's where the pigmen sleep too."

"*Zombie* pigmen," Porkins reminded her.

"Sorry," said Sally. "No villagers are allowed in there. Well, apart from the witch. If we go near it, the pigmen chase us off. I mean *zombie* pigmen, sorry."

"Porkins, you sleep in there for now," said Dave. "You can see what it's like inside, and how easy it would be to get to the portal. Also, find out if Dotty has a way of communicating with Herobrine. The last thing we want is to start a revolution and have him arrive."

"He'll find out eventually, no matter what you do," snapped Adam. "Freeing our village from the pigmen won't do much good if Herobrine can just send more to replace them."

"That's why we have to see what kind of operation Herobrine is running," said Dave. "We have to get inside the Nether."

"We could just build another nether portal," said Carl.

"Good point," said Dave. "Porkins, how do multiple nether portals work—if we built one outside the village, would it bring us to the same portal in the nether as the village one, or would it create a new portal?"

"I think having portals on this side that close to each other, the portal would bring you to the same portal on the nether side as the original portal."

"This is making my head hurt," said Carl. "Nether

portals are too complicated."

"Let's give it some thought, anyway," said Dave. "For now, let's assess what the situation is, and go from there."

"Do I have to stay dressed like a pig?" asked Carl.

"Yes," said Dave.

"Bah," said Carl.

"Don't you mean 'oink'?" said Sally, with a giggle.

Carl did not look happy.

CHAPTER FOUR

The Secret Base

Porkins had never been very good at pretending. When he'd been a baby pigman, back in the Nether, his friends had often put on plays. Whenever Porkins had been cast in a part, everyone told him what a terrible actor he was.

Nonetheless, Porkins was giving pretending to be a zombie his best shot.

"Rrurk!" he grunted as he walked past some zombie pigmen.

"Rrurk!" they grunted back.

Those poor chaps, thought Porkins, looking at the zombie pigmen. They were just mindless creatures now, with no will of their own.

Doing his best zombie walk, Porkins headed towards the nether brick building in the center of town. It was a large building, much larger than the wooden houses that surrounded it, and there were about ten zombie pigmen outside standing guard.

"Rrurk rrurk!" Porkins said to the zombie pigmen, as he walked towards the entrance.

For a second Porkins worried that the zombie pigmen would stop him, but they didn't, so he just walked straight through.

Inside the lobby of the building, zombie pigmen were wandering about aimlessly or just standing still. There were torches on the walls and several iron doors with switches. Some of the pigmen were asleep on the ground.

They just do nothing until they're given orders, thought Porkins. *They're little more than robots.*

Suddenly one of the iron doors sprang open and Dotty the witch marched across the room.

"Out my way!" she said, shoving Porkins.

"Er, rrurk rrurk!" said Porkins.

Dotty pressed a switch and disappeared through another iron door. It changed shut behind her.

Porkins decided to have a snoop round the room that Dotty had just left. None of the other pigmen were paying attention to him, so he just pressed the switch, then walked through the door.

He walked down a corridor lit by torches, then at the end of it he found himself in a room with a nether portal in the middle. Scattered around the room were tables with scraps of parchment on them.

Porkins thought about just going through the nether

portal, but he imagined that on the other side there would be more zombie pigmen guards, and maybe some witches. But then a thought struck him—he was disguised as a zombie pigman; he could go where he wanted. If any of the witches found him, they'd just think he'd wandered into the wrong area.

Ok, thought Porkins. *Here goes.*

He stepped forward into the portal. It shimmered for a second, and then he was inside a corridor made of iron blocks.

Is this the Nether? he wondered. But before he could investigate further, two zombie pigman marched up to him angrily, swinging their golden swords. Porkins ran back inside the portal.

When he emerged back on the other side, he rushed down the nether brick corridor towards the door, but before he could get there, Dotty opened it.

"What are you doing in here?" she snapped. "These doors are meant to keep you idiots out. Come on, back you go."

She grabbed him roughly and pushed him out into the lobby area. The door slammed shut behind her.

So the witches have built some kind of iron structure in the Nether, Porkins thought. *I must tell Dave and the other chaps.*

Suddenly the door swung open again.

"Actually," said Dotty, grabbing Porkins and guiding him back into the portal room, "you can make yourself useful. I need you to deliver my status report to Isabella."

She handed him a piece of paper.

"You got that, idiot?" Dotty asked him. "Bring this... to Isabella."

"Roink roink!" said Porkins.

"Yes, yes," said Dotty impatiently, and she shoved him into the portal. There was a brief shimmer and then he was back inside the iron corridor once more. The two zombie pigman guards marched up to him again, but he waved his piece of paper at them.

"Rrrurk!" said Porkins.

That seemed to satisfy the guards, and they stood down and let him pass.

Porkins walked forward into the corridor. Running down it were two powered rails, and there was a large chest with the word 'minecarts' above it.

One track must run left and the other right, thought Porkins.

There were more signs too, with arrows next to them. There were signs that pointed to things such as 'Barracks' and 'Armory', but also signs with place names on then, each with an arrow pointing either left or right. Pointing right there were two signs with red writing on them: 'Headquarters' and 'Emperor Herobrine'.

Herobrine. Even the name was enough to make Porkins's heart stop in his chest. Herobrine had betrayed the pigmen and turned them into zombies. There was no-one Porkins hated more in the world, and if he took a minecart to the right, he could go see him.

And then what, you silly chap? thought Porkins to himself. Herobrine would probably be incredibly well guarded, and even if Porkins got past the guards he'd have to face Herobrine. He'd seen how powerful Herobrine was: he wouldn't stand a chance.

Porkins unfolded the piece of paper that Dotty had given him and had a look. The contents were fairly boring, it was basically a summary of how many mines had been set up around the village, how big they were, and if there had been any sign of Dave the villager or a stronghold.

Porkins decided the best thing to do was just deliver the piece of paper. He assumed that 'Headquarters' was where this Isabella would be, whoever she was. He opened the chest and pulled out a tiny minecart. When he laid it down on the tracks it grew to full size, so he hopped inside and it zoomed off.

"Waaaa!" yelled Porkins. He'd never ridden in a minecart before, and was amazed at how fast it was. He sped down the iron corridor, rushing past nether portal after nether portal, all guarded by pigmen. The nether portals had signs above them: 'Tree Town', 'Sheepburg',

'Villagertropolis', and many more. The pigmen had built a huge network to help them travel easily from place to place, Porkins realized. No wonder they'd taken over so quickly.

Suddenly the corridor ended, and the rail track sped Porkins across a huge iron bridge in the middle of the nether. Below he could see a sea of lava, stretching out in every direction, and high above him he could see the cavernous netherrack ceiling. He also got his first proper look at the iron building: it was a huge rectangle, with tunnels and bridges leading off to other huge rectangles.

With their minecarts they'll be able to travel anywhere they want in minutes, Porkins thought. He knew that distance in the Nether was different from distance in the overworld. A short minecart journey in the Nether could be a journey of miles in the overworld.

In the distance he could see several half-finished buildings, with pigmen working on them. It looked like Herobrine and the witches were trying to cover the whole of the Nether with their portals.

The bridge Porkins was on was leading towards another huge iron building. Standing around the entrance were more zombie pigmen guards. Porkins's cart zipped through the entrance, and he found himself traveling down another corridor. He sped past more portals, each with names on signs above them.

Suddenly Porkins's cart hit a block, coming to a stop. He was in a room with several minecart tracks leading off in different directions. One was labeled 'To Emperor Herobrine: Senior Witches Only!'. Porkins again had to resist the urge to go straight there.

I'll be back for you, Herobrine old chap, he thought. *You mark my words!*

Instead he placed his cart on the route labeled 'To Headquarters', and sped off once more. His cart traveled down another iron corridor, but that soon ended and the minecart led straight across the barren wasteland of the Nether. There were pigmen all around, putting down iron blocks.

Looks like they're still building this part of the corridor, thought Porkins.

Ahead he could see a castle, which looked like it was made of cobblestone. That was where the minecart track was taking him. As he got closer he could see witches in the windows, all wearing the blue robes that witches loyal to Herobrine wore.

THUNK! The Minecart hit a block right outside the castle, coming to a sudden stop. The entrance was a big open archway, with a sign saying 'Headquarters' above it. A horde of pigmen ran over to Porkins, surrounding him and grunting angrily.

"Get back, you fools," said a bored-sounding voice.

The pigmen all backed off, and a witch strode up to Porkins.

"What have you got for me?" she asked.

"Rrurk rrurk!" said Porkins, handing her the scrap of paper.

The witch took a look. "No surprise there," she said. "Alright, follow me. The boss might have a message for you to bring back."

The witch walked into the castle, Porkins following behind. Inside, witches were working away, most of them writing things or giving orders to pigmen. On one wall was a huge map of the overworld. As Porkins got closer he saw that it was actually lots of normal sized maps stuck together.

"Any report from Villagertropolis?" a witch yelled across the room.

"The siege is still going on," another witch yelled back. "The last report mentioned something about a robot army turning up."

"Well, send more pigmen," the first witch said. "We need that city."

The witch Porkins was following suddenly stopped.

"Wait here," she told him, and she disappeared into a room, closing the wooden door behind her.

There was so much going on in the castle—witches and pigmen going to and fro, witches shouting orders across the room—but Porkins tried his best to see or hear anything that might be useful.

"Has there been any more word from the boss?" one witch asked.

"What, Isabella? Weren't you there at the meeting this morning?" another witch replied.

"No," said the first witch. "Not Lady Isabella. I'm talking about Lord Herobrine."

As she said *Herobrine* she shivered. It could have been his imagination, but Porkins could have sworn that the room got a bit colder.

"Nothing for days," said the other witch. "And anyway, he calls himself *Emperor* now, so make sure you don't use the wrong title. No, the *Emperor* normally keeps himself to himself, unless he has something to say. I doubt we'll hear much from him until we find a stronghold or that Dave."

The first witch suddenly gave Porkins a funny look.

"Are you listening to us, piggy?" she snapped.

"Don't be a fool," said the other witch. "These pigmen are nothing but brainless husks now. As long as Isabella has that golden staff, they'll do whatever we say."

Golden staff. The words made Porkins think back to Trotter, the evil pigman who had used a magical staff that Herobrine had given him to control the zombie pigmen.

That's how the witches can control zombie pigmen,

35

thought Porkins. *They have Herobrine's staff!*

The witches had mentioned that a witch called Isabella now had the staff, and, sure enough, as Porkins looked around the room he saw a sign that said 'Isabella's Quarters: Restricted Access.'

That staff is here, Porkins thought. *If we can capture it or destroy it, the witches won't have control of the zombie pigmen anymore. We can jolly well stop this invasion!*

"We've found that pigmen village!" a witch yelled as she ran into the castle, waving a scrap of paper. "Shall we prepare an invasion force?"

"Why bother?" said a witch. "We've still got plenty of the Emperor's potion. Let's just turn them into zombies."

Porkins remembered the green liquid that Trotter had had. He'd tried to use it on Porkins and his friends, but instead it had gone over him, and turned him into a zombie.

"Right, you," said a voice. Porkins turned round. It was the bored witch who'd led him inside the castle. She passed him a piece of paper.

"Deliver this back to Dotty," she said. "Come on, what you waiting for? Go!"

"Roink!" said Porkins, and he lurched off, doing his best zombie impression.

He placed a minecart down, climbed into it, and it

sped along the track once more. He took a look at the paper, but there was nothing much of interest on it, just orders for Dotty to dig more pits, and dig them faster.

CHAPTER FIVE
Dave Makes a Plan

That evening, Porkins came to see Dave and Carl, to tell them what he'd found out.

"Interesting," said Dave, when Porkins had finished. "So all the control the witches have over the pigmen is because of that staff."

"Exactly," said Porkins. "We destroy that staff and this invasion is finished!"

"You make it sound so easy," said Carl, rolling his eyes.

They were in Sally's home, on the edge of town. Sally lived with Adam, who, Dave had been surprised to find out, was her husband. Even though the two of them argued and disagreed a lot, they seemed to love each other. Or at least tolerate each other.

Dave and Carl had spent the day with Sally and Adam, talking through possible plans of attack. Dave had dug underneath Sally and Adam's house, creating a secret cellar where they could build armor and weapons, and, hopefully, train the villagers to fight.

The only trouble was, all the diamond and iron the villagers had—and everything they dug up in the mines—was always taken back to the Nether by the pigmen. So there wasn't anything to actually build armor and weapons with. Dave had been given a lot of materials when he'd left Cool Island, so he'd used these to make as many weapons as he could, but it wasn't much.

One thing the village did have was trees—plenty of trees. So Dave had decided that tomorrow he and Carl were going to sneak off and get loads of wood, so they could build wooden swords for the villagers. There were herds of cows nearby, so they were going to get as much leather as they could to make armor. It wasn't as good as having iron and diamond, but it would have to do.

"So if this magic staff is as powerful as you say, why don't you just grab it the next time you're sent to the Nether?" asked Adam. He and Sally had joined the conversation too, which was taking place in their kitchen.

"Don't be stupid, Adam" said Sally. "You really think the witches would just leave the staff unguarded?"

"There were a lot of zombie pigmen chaps at that castle," said Porkins sadly. "And we don't know how easy it is to destroy the staff. It might just take a blow from a sword, or it might be more difficult."

"We could always throw it in lava," said Carl. "Lava normally destroys most things. Well, apart from Herobrine, of course. We all saw what happened when *he* fell in lava."

Dave stood up from his chair, walking over and looking out of the window at the night sky.

"I think I'm starting to come up with a plan," he said. "To defeat the witches and end Herobrine's invasion, we need to break their control over the pigmen."

"*Zombie* pigmen," said Porkins.

"Sorry, Porkins," said Dave. "Zombie pigmen."

"Yes, we know all this," said Adam, "but how do you intend to do that?"

"I'm coming to that," said Dave. "One advantage we have over the witches is that they don't know that we know about the magic staff. From what Porkins has told us, it seems that the castle is guarded well, but not *too* well. With a small force we should be able to overwhelm their defenses and get the staff. The trouble we have is that as soon as we attack the castle, they'd send hundreds of zombie pigmen to defend it. They have minecart tracks, so they can easily send more troops from elsewhere."

"Are you going to tell us your plan or not?" said Adam.

"Let the man speak, Adam, for goodness sake!" said Sally. "Carry on, Dave."

"Ok," said Dave, "So what we need to do is make sure the zombie pigmen are too busy to come to defend the castle. We need to launch as many attacks as we can at the same time—not just at Greenleaf, but in as many of the occupied towns and villages as possible. The witches and zombie pigmen will be so busy fighting rebellions, that they won't be able to send reinforcements to the castle."

"How are we going to do that?" said Adam.

"We need to send envoys to as many settlements as possible," said Dave. "Sally, can you provide me with a list of nearby towns and villages, and maps that say how to get to them?"

"I sure can," she grinned.

"Good," said Dave. "Then we arrange a date, and we all launch rebellions at the same time. Herobrine's forces will be overwhelmed."

"One question," said Carl, "if everything goes to plan and we destroy the magic staff and defeat the witches, what next? What do we do about Herobrine?"

The room went silent.

"Can't we all go and attack him?" said Sally. "I know he's meant to be powerful, but if we defeat the witches and the pigs first, we'll easily be able to beat him."

"I'm not so sure, old bean," said Porkins. "As Carl was saying, we've seen the blighter survive falling into lava. I'm not sure he *can* be killed."

"Herobrine is powerful," said Dave, "but without his army, his invasion will be over. We'll destroy his base in the Nether, we'll destroy his portals, and then there won't be anything he can do."

"Except come and destroy us all," said Carl.

"Yes," said Dave, "except for that."

CHAPTER SIX

The Plan Begins

The next day, they started to put the plan into motion.

Dave, Sally and Adam were forced by the zombie pigmen to go to work in one of the pits, but when they were there they started spreading the word about the rebellion, and recruited some of the villagers to be envoys to go and spread the word to other settlements.

The envoys sneaked out of the village that night to go to other towns and villages nearby. Dave and Sally had decided that the rebellion should take place in two weeks' time, to make sure there was enough time to get things sorted.

Every night, villagers would sneak over to Sally and Adam's house, and in the basement Dave would teach them to sword fight. Dave was reminded of his own time training with Ripley back in Snow Town. It didn't seem that long ago, but now Dave was the trainer. He'd enlarged the basement, digging it out so that it was much bigger than the house above. In fact he'd made it so big that it went underneath other houses in the village, allowing the villagers to sneak back and forth without the pigmen seeing.

Porkins and Carl kept themselves busy too. Carl sneaked out at night in his iron golem suit, guarding a group of villagers as they cut down trees for wood and dug up as much iron as they could find. Then they'd sneak it back to Sally and Adam's basement where it would be smelted and turned into weapons and armor. Then, during the day, Carl would put more pink makeup on and go back to pretending to be a pig.

Porkins kept pretending to be a zombie, living in the barracks with all the other zombie pigmen. It was a bittersweet experience, as he was, finally, surrounded by his own kind again, but they were mindless zombies.

He kept thinking about what he'd heard in the castle in the Nether: about the pigman village that the witches had found, and their plan to turn all the pigmen into zombies. He hoped that Dave's rebellion would defeat the witches before that could happen.

So everyone in the village was doing their part. They'd spread the word to other settlements, and they were training for the fight themselves. Everything was going to plan. But, as with many plans, there was something that hadn't been considered: that one of their own would betray them.

Adam had disliked Dave and his friends from the start. Since he was a baby villager, Adam had always followed the rules. He'd always done what he'd been told and had never been in trouble, but now he was being asked to be part of a *rebellion!*

To Adam, there was nothing wrong with working in the mines, even if they were being forced to do it by the pigmen. It was good, honest work. In Adam's opinion, many of his fellow villagers were far too lazy anyway, and a bit of hard work would do them good.

So as his wife and his fellow villagers prepared to fight the pigmen, Adam grew increasingly uneasy. In his opinion, rebelling against the pigmen would only lead to trouble. Better that the villagers kept doing what they were told and behaved themselves.

When he said as much to his wife one evening over dinner, she laughed in his face.

"Don't be such a coward, dear," she said. "Why don't you go down to the basement tonight and practice with the others? I don't think I've even ever seen you hold a sword."

"You never *will* see me hold a sword," snapped Adam. "Villagers aren't meant to be warriors. This *Dave* is putting ridiculous ideas into everyone's heads. Villagers are meant to behave themselves. Maybe do the odd bit of trading. Fighting is for Steves!"

"You know, Dave's fought alongside Steve," said Sally, taking a bite of chicken. "He's a villager, and he's fought with Steve. He's proof that we don't have to be who we were born to be. We can be whoever we want."

"Bah," said Adam.

That night, Adam tossed and turned in bed, unable to decide what to do. But by morning he'd made his decision. He got up as quietly as he could, so as to not wake his wife, and left his house. The morning air was crisp and there was no-one around. He walked straight over to the nether brick building, where he was confronted by four zombie pigman guards.

"I need to speak to your boss," he told them. "I need to speak to Dotty."

CHAPTER SEVEN
Porkins's Dilemma

Porkins couldn't stop thinking about the pigman village.

He was lying on the floor in the pigman barracks. The zombie pigmen around him were all snoring and grunting, but that wasn't what was keeping him awake.

What should I do? he wondered, for the thousandth time. Every since Gammon had told him that there was a pigman village, back on Cool Island, Porkins hadn't been able to stop thinking about it. He'd always assumed that he was the last non-zombie pigman left, but now he knew that wasn't true. And now the witches were plotting to turn the pigmen in a village they'd found into zombies. Porkins didn't know if this pigman village was the same as Gammon's one, but he knew that he couldn't just do nothing. He couldn't let more of his people get turned into zombies by Herobrine.

Eventually he made up his mind. He got up, then tiptoed over to a certain block in the corner of the room.

Dave and the other villagers had built secret tunnels underneath the village, so the villagers could sneak around without the pigmen knowing. They'd even built one that went underneath the nether brick building. The passageway was underneath the pigman dormitory where Porkins slept, underneath one of the nether brick floor blocks.

Porkins smashed the block with his fist, jumped inside the passageway, then replaced the block. The pigmen in the dormitory above would be none the wiser.

The passageway was only small—two bricks high, one brick wide—and lit by the occasional torch along its dirt walls. As Porkins traveled he passed entrances to other passageways, with signs such as 'To Mrs Bogg's House' or 'Secret Armory'. It reminded Porkins of the iron tunnels in the Nether.

He followed the signs to 'Sally and Adam's House', which led to a ladder. He climbed the ladder, opened a trap door and found himself in the cellar that Dave had built underneath the house. There were weapons lying about the place, and item frames with apples in them attached to the mud walls, which the villagers had been using for archery practice. Dave was the only person there, swinging his sword and practicing his technique.

"Hey Porkins," Dave said. "Any news? Or have you just come to train?"

"Neither," said Porkins nervously. "Dave, old bean, I need to ask you something. I know you need me here, but... when I was inside that castle in the Nether I heard the witches talking about a village of pigmen. Normal pigmen, not these zombie blighters. The witches are planning to turn the poor chaps into zombies. They might be the last normal pigmen in the world, apart from me, and I need to go and help them. Do I... do I have your blessing?"

"Oh Porkins," said Dave. And to Porkins's' surprise Dave went over and gave him a hug. "Of course you do. I know how much this must mean to you. Go—go and save your people. Do you want me to go with you?"

"I can't ask you that, dear chap," said Porkins, wiping a tear from his eye. "This village needs you. Besides, I'm the only one who can sneak into the Nether. When I'm pretending to be a zombie, they'll be none the wiser."

"Ok," said Dave, "but stay safe."

"I will," said Porkins. "And if I find the pigmen in time I'll rally the chaps to join the revolution as well. Herobrine won't stand a chance!"

"He certainly won't," grinned Dave.

"You really think we stand a chance against Herobrine?"

It was Carl. He'd climbed down the ladder from Sally

and Adam's house above.

"Don't get me wrong," continued Carl, "I like these villagers. And that's me talking—the creeper who hates everyone. But is this revolution idea really going to work?"

"It has to," said Dave. "It sounds like Herobrine isn't going to stop until he conquers the whole world."

"Come on," said Carl. "You know that's not what Herobrine really wants."

Porkins was confused. "What does the blighter want then?" he asked.

"What he's always wanted," said Carl. "He wants to get to the End. That's why he's told everyone to be on the lookout for Dave; that's why he's digging all these pits. He knows that the only way to reach the End is to find an ender portal. He's forcing the villagers to dig, hoping that they'll eventually find a stronghold. But he also knows that Dave found a way to *find* strongholds, so Herobrine wants Dave as well. From what we've seen of his power, he could have conquered the world ages ago, if that's what he wanted, but he doesn't care about that. It's a means to an end. Or, rather, a means to *the* End."

Dave sat down, rubbing his forehead with his hands.

"You're right," he said. "Maybe... maybe I should just hand myself over to him. If I hand myself over to Herobrine and tell him about the eyes of ender, maybe he'll leave everyone alone."

"No," said Porkins. "Remember what your grandmother told you, in your head—Herobrine must *not* find his way to the End, or terrible things will happen!"

"Oh yeah," said Carl. "I forgot about your magic grandma and her crazy talking-in-your-head thing."

"I wish we could talk to her properly," sighed Dave. "Find out what's really going on with Herobrine. I've been trying to speak to her in my head again, but I think it only works when those good witches are nearby."

"Talking to your grandma in your head is the first sign of madness," said Carl. "Everyone knows that."

"You'd better go, Porkins," Dave said. "Find your people in time. Save them."

"I will," said Porkins. "I will."

Porkins said his goodbyes to Dave and Carl, then went back down into the secret passage. He returned to the nether brick building, where the zombie pigmen were still asleep, then made his way to the portal. Thankfully, it was unguarded.

As soon as he walked through into the Nether, two angry pigmen guards rushed up to him.

"Rrurk rrurk!" said Porkins, showing them a scrap of paper he'd taken from Dotty's desk. It was blank, but, as Porkins suspected, the zombie pigmen were too stupid to know any different, and they stood back and let him pass.

Porkins looked up at all the signs on the iron wall, all pointing to different settlements.

Which one is the pigman village? he wondered. Then he saw a sign saying:

'Little Bacon.'

Ah, he thought. *That's probably the one.* He took out a minecart from the treasure chest, then sped off down the powered rail.

CHAPTER EIGHT
The Night Before

It was the night before the rebellion, and Dave was giving the villagers one last training session.

"And swing... and parry... and swing and swing!"

He stood at the front of the room with them all behind him, copying his moves. They were in the huge basement underneath Sally and Adam's house.

From the back of the room, Dave could hear the twanging of arrows as the villagers on archery duty practiced their shots. Carl was training them. Well, at least he was meant to be training them. What he was really doing was yelling things like "shoot straight, you dirt-brained idiot!" and "a sheep could aim better than you!" How useful this 'training' was to the archers Dave wasn't sure.

Dave finished his sword lesson, then let the villagers practice by themselves for a bit. As he watched them practicing their sword techniques with each other, he felt a great sense of pride. A few days ago they hadn't known one end of a sword from the other, but now they were ready for battle. Or at least he hoped they were.

There was almost a full set of iron armor for every villager now, and an iron sword. Some of them would have to make do with leather armor and wooden swords, as Carl and his diggers hadn't managed to find quite as much material as they may have hoped, but Dave made sure to give the worst weapons and armor to the best fighters, as the worst fighters would need all the protection they could get: Dave had even given some of them diamond armor, using up the last of his diamonds.

For himself he took leather armor and a wooden sword, to lead by example. He would have much preferred diamond, but he knew that if he went out in diamond armor with a diamond sword, it wouldn't be very inspiring for his troops.

Carl had sneaked his iron golem suit into the basement the night before. It was currently propped up in a corner, and Dave knew that Carl was itching to get inside it again and fight.

That morning two of the envoys had returned from their quest to stir up the nearby towns and villages against the pigmen. The envoys were pleased to report that between them they'd convinced six settlements to join the fight. Disappointingly they hadn't managed to get

Villagertropolis on side, which was a shame as it had by far the biggest population. According to the envoys, the city had closed its gates, and no-one was coming in or out. Whether it was still under the control of the pigmen, they didn't know.

So Greenleaf and at least six other settlements were ready to launch their attack tomorrow. *This is going to work,* thought Dave happily.

As Dave was lost in his thoughts, Sally and Adam came down the ladder from their house.

"This is so exciting!" said Sally, giving Dave a hug. "We're really going to teach those pigmen a lesson!"

"*Zombie* pigman," said Dave with a smile. "Porkins would never forgive me if he heard we'd just been calling them *pigmen.*"

"Hmmph," said Adam. "Whatever they are, we don't stand a chance. You should just give up this silly plan. Villagers aren't meant to be warriors, how many times do I have to tell you all?"

"Oh do be quiet, Adam," said Sally. "You'll be eating your words tomorrow, when we win."

"We'll see," said Adam. "Somehow I don't think tomorrow is going to go exactly as you've planned."

And he stormed off, climbing back up the ladder.

"Sorry about him, Dave," said Sally. "He's a good man

really, it's just... like all of us in the village, he was raised to believe that villagers aren't meant to be heroes."

"I was raised that way too," said Dave. "Let's prove to him that he's wrong."

Dave turned to the other villagers, who were still practicing their archery and swordplay.

"Ok everyone, let's stop now," he said. "We've got a big day ahead of us tomorrow. Remember, we attack at first light—so be ready. Get some sleep, you're going to want to be well rested."

The villagers all trundled off, back through the secret tunnels to their own homes. They were in good spirits, Dave was pleased to see, all of them eager for the fight.

Dave went over the battle plans in his head a few more times, then lay down in bed. He and Carl were staying in separate beds in Sally and Adam's spare room.

We're going to win, was his last thought before drifting off. But that night his dreams were full of doubt. He dreamed of Herobrine's empty white eyes. *You can't defeat me,* those eyes seemed to be saying. *No-one can defeat me...*

CHAPTER NINE
Little Bacon

Porkins walked out of the portal and found himself in an unfamiliar biome. It was night, but he could make out tall trees all around him. He could barely see the sky; it was blocked from view by a canopy of leaves.

In the darkness he saw a couple of small creatures staring back at him, their eyes reflecting the moonlight.

"*Mew!*" one of them said.

"Hello, little chaps," said Porkins, walking towards them. The creatures immediately scampered off.

Which way is the village? wondered Porkins. The nether portal behind him was in the middle of nowhere. Back in the Nether the sign above the portal had said "Little Bacon", but there was no sign of anyone on the other side.

Porkins thought back to what he'd heard in the witches' castle. From the sounds of it, the witches had found the pigman village but hadn't conquered it yet.

He started walking through the trees, looking for any sign of life. Occasionally he'd catch sight of one of the little mew-ing creatures, but as soon as they saw him looking at them they'd run away.

Eventually he saw some faint lights up ahead. He kept walking and eventually realized that the lights were coming from up in the trees. As he got closer he started to hear voices as well, and eventually he saw, to his shock, that there were *buildings* in the trees.

That's the village! he realized. He could just make out a few faint figures moving about, but it was so dark and they were so high up that he couldn't see them properly.

At the bottom of one of the trees was a ladder. Next to the ladder was a sign:

'Little Bacon"

Porkins began to climb the ladder. It was a long climb, and when he got nearer the top he noticed something strange: all the voices he'd heard earlier had stopped.

Maybe they all go to bed at the same time? he thought.

When he reached the top he found himself on a wooden platform. The village was a series of wooden platforms attached to trees, connected to each other by wooden bridges. The houses were all small and made of wood too. There were torches burning, but no sign of life.

"Hello?" Porkins called out. "Hello chaps, is there

anyone here?"

"Put your hands in the air and drop your weapon."

Porkins turned towards the sound of the voice. A pigman was aiming a bow and arrow at him from the roof of one of the houses. Then he noticed another pigman. And another. There were at least ten pigmen, all aiming at him.

"Hello chaps!" said Porkins. "It's so good to finally meet you!"

"He's one of those zombies," said one of the pigmen. "We should just kill him."

"The zombies can't talk though," said another.

"Oh no," said Porkins, realizing the misunderstanding. "This is just makeup!"

He wiped off some of the zombie makeup with his hand.

"I TOLD YOU TO DROP YOUR WEAPON!" the first pigman shouted.

Porkins quickly dropped his golden sword.

"My... my name's Porkins," said Porkins nervously. This wasn't quite the positive reception he'd been hoping for. "I've come to warn you, you're all in grave danger."

"What kind of danger?" asked one of the pigman.

"The fiend Herobrine has started taking over the world," said Porkins. "He has witches and zombie pigmen working for him, and they know you're here. They want to turn all of you into zombies too!"

"Ok," said the pigman. "We'll take you to see the village elder. But if we find out you're lying to us, we're throwing you off the top of this tree."

"Oh crumbs," said Porkins.

CHAPTER TEN
Elder Crispy

Before Porkins knew what was happening, a big pigman grabbed him and roughly pushed him along, guiding him across a bridge towards the biggest house in the tree village. It was the only house with two stories, and it had two guards outside.

"Wake Elder Crispy," said the big pigman to one of the guards.

Porkins was guided inside, into a small chamber with a wooden throne at one end. On the wall were paintings, many of them of events that Porkins recognized: famous events in pigman history.

A tall pigman with a huge barrel chest walked down the stairs, into the chamber.

"So," said the barrel-chested pigman. "Who might you be? And why shouldn't I throw you out of my tree?"

"He says the village is in danger, Elder," said the big pigman who'd brought Porkins inside.

"Silence, Ricco," said the Elder. "I want the stranger to tell me the story in his own words. I will determine whether or not he speaks true. And if he is false, he'll—"

"—be thrown out of the tree, yes, yes, I know," said Porkins. "Listen old bean, time really is of the essence here, so I'll make this quick."

The chamber had got busy now, Porkins saw. The other pigmen had all squeezed their way inside, eager to hear what he had to say. There were even baby pigman. That made Porkins smile: he had thought he might never see a baby pigman again.

"Ok," said Porkins, "here goes..."

He took a deep breath.

"Herobrine is taking over the world invading all the villages and towns and cities he can find with his army of zombie pigmen and witches and now he's found your village so he's sending his army here and he's going to turn you all into zombies to be his slaves so we need to act fast and tomorrow there's going to be a revolution and we're going to rise up against Herobrine and the witches so we could do with your help as we want to create a distraction so we can sneak into the castle in the Nether that the witches use for their base so we can destroy the magic staff that lets them control the zombie pigman as without it they'll have no army anymore."

"Sorry, old chap," said an elderly pigman, "I didn't

have my hearing aid turned on. Could you repeat that?"

"Ah, ok..." said Porkins, struggling to get his breath back. "Herobrine is taking over the world invading all the villages and towns and cities he can find with his army of zombie pigmen and witches and now he's found your village so he's sending his army here and he's going to turn you all into zombies to be his slaves so we need to act fast and tomorrow there's going to be a revolution and we're going to rise up against Herobrine and the witches so we could do with your help as we want to create a distraction so we can sneak into the castle in the Nether that the witches use for their base so we can destroy the magic staff that lets them control the zombie pigman as without it they'll have no army anymore."

"That was better, thank you kindly," said the elderly pigman.

"Herobrine," said Elder Crispy, his voice gruff. "We have heard stories of him. It is a long time since we left the Nether, but we know what happened to the pigman who remained there. We thought they were all turned to zombies, but here you are."

"Yes, here I am," said Porkins. "By the way I met a chap who came from your village, I think. Went by the name of Gammon."

Elder Crispy spat on the floor. "Gammon was a criminal," he growled. "He and two others from our village

63

were exiled months ago for their crimes."

"Ah, that makes a lot of sense," said Porkins. "He seemed like a good egg... but then he tried to kill me and my friends, which wasn't very nice."

"Stop babbling," said Elder Crispy. "You tell us that we're in danger, but as you can tell we are fierce warriors. We've defended our village from villains in the past, and we can defend it again."

"I can see that," said Porkins. "It's clear to me that you're all pretty robust chaps. I'm sure if the witches and zombie blighters came here you'd give them a darn good hiding. Which is why I'd like you to join the revolution. My friends will need all the help they can get to win their battle tomorrow. Most of the villager chaps have never fought before, so having some seasoned warriors like you and your people on side would be just the ticket."

"*Just the ticket,*" said Elder Crispy, with a smile. "You sound just like one of the old folk, the ones who first left the Nether all those years ago."

"Yes, you jolly well do," said the elderly pigman with a smile.

"As you can tell," said Elder Crispy, "the way we speak has changed. When we left the Nether, our people traveled for many years. The way was hard and we had to become hard too."

"I'm sorry to hear that," said Porkins. "But please do come and join the villager chaps in the battle tomorrow. Together we can give Herobrine a thrashing!"

Elder Crispy sighed.

"What is your name, stranger?"

"Porkins," said Porkins.

"Porkins," said Elder Crispy, "you seem like a good pig, but this is not our fight. If the villagers want to go to war, that is their business. My people keep to ourselves. That is how we've survived so long. That is why we chose to live in this jungle, far away from civilization."

"But the villagers need your help!" insisted Porkins.

"And did the villagers come to your aid when your people were turned to zombies?" asked Elder Crispy.

Porkins tried to think of a response, but he couldn't.

"I thought not," said Elder Crispy. "Porkins, I wish you well, but the pigmen of Little Bacon will not be joining your fight. Ricco, Nathan, please escort Porkins out of the village.

The big pigman Ricco and a normal-sized one grabbed Porkins, and gently led him out of the chamber, pushing past the crowd of pigmen.

"Please help," Porkins begged, looking round at the faces of his fellow pigmen. "If we don't all stick together, villains like Herobrine will keep on winning!"

They led Porkins out of the Elder's house and back to the ladder that led down the tree.

"Sorry," said the normal-sized pigman, who Porkins assumed must be Nathan. "If it was up to me I'd help you, but I can't go against the wishes of Elder Crispy. He's been a good leader for our people."

"Good luck," added Ricco.

Porkins made his way sadly down the ladder.

That could have gone better, he thought miserably.

CHAPTER ELEVEN

Attack!

Dave couldn't sleep. There was still hours to go until sunrise, but he had too much on his mind. He suspected that many of the other villagers must be feeling the same way: too excited and scared to sleep.

He went over the plan again in his head. As soon as the sun began to rise the archers would sneak onto the rooftops of houses all round the village. Then the swordsmen would charge into the nether brick building, taking out the zombie pigmen and capturing Dotty before she could escape to the Nether and raise the alarm.

From the intel that Porkins had given them, Dave knew exactly where the zombie pigmen all slept, so it would be easy to take them by surprise. Dotty was a different matter, as she'd surely try to use the nether portal as soon as she realized the villagers were rising up. So Dave had arranged a surprise for her: some of the villagers had dug a tunnel directly underneath the nether portal (they knew where it was thanks to Porkins), and once the attack began they would dig up into the room above and surround the portal, making sure she couldn't use it.

The other villages and towns that had agreed to join the revolution would be launching their attacks at sunrise too, Dave knew. Then once they had defeated the pigmen in their settlements they would march into the Nether, fighting the zombie pigmen on their home turf. Meanwhile Dave, Carl and a select group would make their way to the witches' castle, storm it, take the magical staff and then destroy it.

It was a solid plan, but Dave couldn't help but worry. He knew from experience that even the best-laid plans could go wrong.

"Having trouble sleeping?" muttered Carl from his bed on the other side of the room.

Dave sat up in his own bed. "Yeah," he said. "Just worrying about the morning."

"It'll be fine," said Carl. "You'll have me there to protect you. You've seen how awesome I am in my iron golem suit. Those pigmen won't know what's hit them."

Suddenly Dave heard a sound. A *snorting* sound outside of the window.

"What was that?" he whispered.

"What was what?" said Carl.

Dave reached over and slowly, quietly grabbed his

wooden sword.

"I think there's a pigman outside," he said. "Maybe more than one."

"So what?" whispered Carl. "They own the village, for now, they can go wherever they like."

Carl was right, Dave knew, but normally at night the pigmen stayed near the nether brick building, or around the edge of the town to stop anyone from escaping. They never wandered near the houses.

"Prepare yourself," said Dave.

"For what?" said Carl.

SMASH!!! A zombie pigman smashed through the glass pane of the window, leaning through and swinging his golden sword about. Behind it, Dave could see a whole hoard of zombie pigmen, all trying to get in.

"Waaaa!" said Carl.

"Come on, to the basement," said Dave. "Let's get some weapons and your iron suit."

Dave and Carl jumped out of bed and ran through the house. They ran into Sally and Adam's room and shook them awake.

"The pigmen are attacking!" Dave yelled. Then SMASH!!! a zombie pigman smashed his way through their bedroom window.

"They must have found out about our attack!" wailed

Sally. "But how?"

"We can work that out later," said Dave. "They won't know about the basement and the underground passages, so we can get some weapons and regroup there. Come on!"

The four of them ran to the kitchen, then opened the secret trapdoor under the rug, climbing down the ladder that led to the basement. Once they got down there though, it was full of zombie pigmen too.

"Hey, get off that!" yelled Carl. Some of the pigmen were hitting his iron suit with their swords, obviously thinking it was a real golem. "You idiot pigs!"

The pigmen charged at them. From the secret passageways Dave could hear villagers shouting and fighting taking place.

The pigmen knew, he thought desperately. *Someone must have told them!*

"Come on!" said Dave. He ran back towards the ladder that led up to the house, the other three following behind him, but when they got there they saw more pigmen coming down the ladder. Dave drew his sword, ready to fight, but soon the pigmen had surrounded them, snorting angrily.

"Put your sword down, fool," Adam snapped at Dave. "You really think you can take them all on with a wooden blade? We need to surrender."

For once, Dave had to agree with Adam. He dropped

his sword and put his hands up.

"We surrender," he said.

The zombie pigmen marched Dave, Carl, Sally and Adam back up the ladder, then into the town square. All the other villagers were there too, with their hands in the air. The sun was beginning to rise, orange light spreading across the village. It was a beautiful sight, but no-one was in the mood to appreciate it.

"What happened, Dave?" one of the villagers asked him, tears in her eyes. "This was meant to be the day we fought back."

"Well, well, well," said a voice. Dave turned and saw Dotty looking down at them from the balcony of the nether brick building. "So your name isn't *Dean* after all? I thought I recognized you, *Dave*."

Dave touched his face. He hadn't drawn on his fake beard.

"So now you know," he said to Dotty.

"Oh, I knew already," grinned Dotty. "The same way I knew about the little invasion you had planned today. You really should be more careful with who you trust."

Adam stepped forward.

"You promised that my wife and I would be allowed to leave unharmed," he said to Dotty. "That was the deal."

"*You?*" gasped Sally, looking at her husband in horror.

"You're the one who betrayed us?"

"It was for your own good," said Adam. "This was a stupid plan. I'm *saving* us, Sally! Lady Dotty has promised that you and I can leave. We can start a new life together somewhere new."

"I'm not going anywhere with you," said Sally. "You disgust me."

"Aww," said Dotty, "that's not very nice. You husband did a very nice thing for you. Adam, you and your wife are free to go."

Adam held out his hand. "Come on, Sally," he said, "let's go."

"No," said Sally.

"Sally, please," begged Adam. "I want to save you!"

"You could have saved me by fighting," said Sally. "You could have helped save us all. But instead you betrayed us, and I never want to see you again."

Adam's mouth fell open in shock. He looked like he wanted to cry.

"Well, are you leaving or not?" said Dotty. "Either leave now, or you can share the same fate as the rest of your pathetic villagers."

Adam looked like he was about to say something, then he sadly walked away.

"Coward," said Sally. She was crying.

"Right," said Dotty, once Adam was gone, "it goes without saying that your revolution is over. Now, my pigmen are going to escort you all into the Nether, and you're all going to be good little villagers and do what you're told. Oh, and you," she said to Dave, "I'll be bringing you to Lord Herobrine myself."

"I thought he was Emperor Herobrine now?" said Carl.

"Of course," said Dotty, with a grin. "Although calling him by the correct title won't save you, little creeper."

Dotty looked down at the zombie pigmen.

"Take our prisoners into the Nether," she told them.

"Not so fast, you dastardly cad!"

Suddenly a golden sword appeared at Dotty's throat. Holding it was a zombie pigman who Dave recognized.

"Porkins!" he said happily.

"The very fellow," grinned Porkins. "Right, you rotter," he said to Dotty, "I'm guessing that these zombie chaps will do whatever you say, so tell them to ruddy well back off!"

"You really think you can stop Lord Herobrine?" laughed Dotty. "We know about your revolution. As we speak my witch sisters will be shutting down all the other rebellions. You're finished."

"You're the one who's finished," said Dave. "You were

going to bring us all into the Nether. Why?"

Dotty grinned. "Once Lord Herobrine learned of the rebellion, he decided that villagers were too much trouble. So he's got bigger plans for all of you."

"And are you going to tell us what those plans are?" said Dave.

"He's going to turn you into zombies," said Dotty. "It's probably happening to all the other villagers right now."

Dave had heard enough. "Right," he said to Dotty, "tell the zombie pigmen to leave the village and get as far away from here as possible. If you don't, Porkins will chop your head off."

"It would be my ruddy pleasure," said Porkins.

Dotty rolled her eyes. "Why does everything with you have to be so dramatic? Ok, piggies, leave the village and get as far away as possible. Go on, go!"

With lots of grunting and snorting the pigmen shuffled off, filing out of the village, into the plains and trees that lay beyond.

"Your army's gone now," said Dave to Dotty, once the zombie pigmen were out of sight.

"The good thing about zombie pigmen is that there's always plenty more," said Dotty. She gave Porkins a nasty grin. "In fact, I've heard of a whole village of normal pigmen living in a jungle biome. Once they're zombies, they can be my new army."

"You shut up!" said Porkins.

Suddenly a lot of things happened at once. Dotty shoved an elbow into Porkins's face. "Ow!" he yelled, and dropped his sword. Dotty grabbed the sword and ran back inside the nether brick building.

"Stop her!" Dave yelled. They all charged into the nether brick building, just in time to see Dotty disappear into the nether portal.

"Now what?" asked Sally.

"We've lost the element of surprise," said Dave, "but if Dotty was telling the truth, all the other villagers who joined our rebellion will be being taken to the Nether to be turned into zombies. So I'm going to go to the Nether, free the villagers and then storm that castle. I can't promise it'll work, but anyone who wants to is welcome to come with me. Anyone who doesn't want to come, I understand. Just make sure you get as far away from the village as possible, before Herobrine's forces come back."

"We're with you, Dave," said Sally. "All of us."

The villagers all cheered.

"Right," said Dave, grinning, "let's get our armor on."

CHAPTER TWELVE

Once More Into the Nether

The villagers gathered in the village square outside of the nether brick building. As Dave stood in front of them, he felt proud. A few days ago they'd been ordinary villagers, but now they were warriors, wearing armor and ready to fight. Carl was there too, in his iron golem suit. Not long ago Carl had tried to avoid fighting whenever he could, but now the creeper was rearing to join the battle.

As Dave stepped forward, the villagers all stopped talking and looked at him.

Oh dear, thought Dave, *do they want me to give a speech?*

His mind went blank. He didn't know what to say.

"Give us a speech, you idiot!" yelled Carl.

"Er, right," said Dave, trying to sound braver than he felt, "we know why we're doing this. We're not fighting just for this village, but for all the other villagers who Herobrine has enslaved. We're fighting for the pigmen, who Herobrine turned into zombies without a care in the world. We're doing this to save the other brave villagers of the rebellion, who right now may be being taken to be turned into zombies as well. So we're going to fight, and we're going to defeat the witches, destroy their base, and kick Herobrine's back side! Who's with me?"

A mighty cheer went up, all the villagers waving their swords or bows in the air. Even Carl was caught up in the excitement, punching the air with his huge iron arms. Porkins was there too, his zombie makeup all washed off and his leather armor back on. He was smiling.

Dave turned towards the nether brick building. "Onwards!" he yelled, marching through the building, the army of villagers marching behind him. He opened the iron door and led them down the corridor to the room with the nether portal. He stepped up into the portal and...

... found himself in an iron corridor. Dave had been in the Nether plenty of times now, but had never seen it like this. The villagers were all coming out of the portal behind him now, so he stepped out of the way.

"Those pigmen have been busy," Dave said to Porkins.

"Oh yes, old bean," said Porkins. "And this stretches on for miles—corridors going in every direction."

Once all the villagers were through, Dave, Porkins, Carl and Sally led the way down the corridor, following the signs that led to the 'Headquarters'. It would have been quicker to travel by minecart, but there were far too many of them, and Dave wanted them to stick together.

"Keep your eye out for an attack," Dave said. "Remember, Dotty will have told them we're coming."

Suddenly Dave spotted something up ahead: minecarts were speeding towards them down the tracks, but they appeared to be empty.

"Porkins," said Dave. "You've got good eyes... what's going on with those minecarts?"

Porkins squinted. Then his mouth dropped open.

"Good gravy!" he gasped. "TNT! The minecarts are all full of TNT!"

Dave could see now that Porkins was right: each cart had a TNT block inside of it.

Panic broke out, all the villagers pushing and shoving. They tried digging at the iron blocks of the walls, but they had no pickaxes and would never get through before the TNT reached them.

What are we going to do? thought Dave. And then he had an idea.

"Archers, get in formation!" Dave yelled.

The archers pushed forward, preparing their bows. Porkins was with them.

"Ok," said Dave, "aim... fire!"

The arrows flew, whizzing through the air and smacking into the TNT blocks, but they didn't explode.

"We need fire!" said Sally. "Flaming arrows destroy TNT!"

"Of course!" said Porkins. "Dave, old bean, give me your flint and iron... and a block of netherrack!"

Dave pulled his flint and iron and the block from his backpack and threw it to Porkins.

"Hurry," Dave said. The minecarts were almost upon them now; in a few seconds they'd be blown to bits.

Porkins placed the netherrack block down and struck the flint and iron across it, setting it alight. Then he strung his bow, dipped the arrow in the fire and let it fly. The arrow's path was true; it flew through the air and hit one of TNT blocks.

KAAAABOOOOOM!!!!!!!

There was a gigantic explosion, the force of it sending Dave and the others flying backwards. But they were alive: Porkins had saved them.

They walked forward to inspect the damage. The corridor had been completely destroyed, leaving a huge chasm with only lava below.

"Well done, Porkins," said Dave. "Everyone, we'll have to take another route.

Then he heard a sound coming from behind them: the sound of hundreds of snorting and grunting pigmen.

"The pigmen are coming!" Dave heard a villager yell.

They were trapped: pigman coming from one end of

the corridor, a fall into lava on the other end.

There was only one thing they could do.

"Fight them!" Dave yelled. "Fight them back!"

The villagers charged forward against the zombie pigmen, sword clashing against sword as they fought. Dave, Carl, Porkins, Sally and the archers were at the back, next to the broken section of the corridor, so they couldn't join the battle; the corridor was too narrow to get through, and it was jam packed with villagers.

"We have to keep moving onwards," Dave said. "They'll keep sending more and more troops at us if we stay still."

He rummaged around in his backpack and pulled out some blocks, any blocks he could find, and threw them to Porkins, Carl and Sally.

"Come on," said Dave, "let's get this corridor rebuilt."

They got to work putting blocks down, rebuilding the broken section of corridor. When they finished it was a mish mash of different blocks, but it was enough; the floor was complete and the walls were two blocks high so no-one would fall over the edge.

"Oh no," Porkins said, the color draining from his face, "more zombies!"

Porkins was right, Dave saw. Coming from up ahead, from the direction the minecarts had come, was another army of zombie pigmen.

"Pigmen behind us, pigmen in front," said Carl. "That's just great."

"*Zombie* pigmen," said Porkins.

"Archers, get in front!" Dave yelled. The archers ran forward, aiming their bows at the zombie pigmen.

"On my mark..." said Dave. He was waiting for the zombie pigmen to get close enough to hit. "Wait for it... FIRE!"

The archers loosed their arrows, and they flew through the air, *poof*ing some of the zombie pigmen.

"Prepare you bows again!" Dave yelled. "And fire!"

More arrows hit more zombie pigmen, taking a lot of them out, but there were still plenty more, charging towards them.

"Archers step back," said Dave, "swordsmen forward."

He could still hear the clatter of battle down the corridor behind him. He hoped the villagers back there were doing ok.

Dave, Carl and the other swordsmen down this end of the corridor stepped forward and drew their blades. The zombie pigmen were almost upon them now.

"For Greenleaf!" Sally yelled.

"For Greenleaf!" The other villagers repeated.

And then the zombie pigmen were upon them. It was chaos: Carl swinging his huge iron arms, swords clashing, archers firing shots. The villagers were trapped in the iron corridor with zombie pigmen coming from either side, fighting for their lives.

All around Dave could hear the familiar *POOF* sound as either a villager or a zombie pigman was slain; he hoped there were more pigmen being slain than villagers, but it was so chaotic that it was hard to keep track.

Dave was fighting as hard as he could, but his wooden sword wasn't doing much good. He spotted a diamond sword on the floor, and for a second he didn't want to pick it up, as he knew it must have been dropped by a slain villager, but then a zombie pigman charged at him and he had no choice. He dropped his wooden blade, grabbed the diamond one and thrust it through the pigman's chest.

Dave had been in battles before, but never one as ferocious as this. It was every man for himself; there was no time to use tactics or clever moves, they just had to fight. And there was nowhere to retreat to either, so they had no choice but to keep fighting.

"We've won!" Dave heard someone yell. He looked around: they were right. All the zombie pigmen were gone. The battle had been so crazy that he hadn't even noticed.

"Grab... grab the best weapons and armor you can," Dave said, struggling to get his breath back. As he looked round he realized how few of them were left. It seemed like less than half the villagers had made it through the battle.

"I know these weapons and armor belonged to your friends, but we need to make sure we're well armed," said Dave. "So kit yourself out."

Dave picked up some diamond armor for himself.

To Dave's relief, Porkins, Carl and Sally had all survived the battle.

"This is all Adam's fault," said Sally angrily. "If he hadn't told the witch our plans, we would have taken them unawares. All these deaths are on his hands."

"Sometimes even the best plans can go wrong," said Dave. "There's no point thinking over what might have been. Even if Adam hadn't told, it probably wouldn't have gone smoothly."

Once the remaining villagers had kitted themselves out with the best weapons and armor that they could find, Dave addresses them once more.

"I'll understand if anyone doesn't want to go on," he said. "This will be probably be the last chance you'll get to turn back, so if anyone wants to leave, now's the time."

None of the villagers wanted to leave. Dave was pleased, but also worried.

Am I just leading them to their doom? he couldn't help but wonder.

"Come on then," he said, "let's go and pay these witches a visit."

CHAPTER THIRTEEN
The Pit

So they marched down the long iron corridor, Dave, Porkins and Carl in the lead. They crossed the open-air bridge that Porkins had crossed before, and the villagers got their first real look at the Nether.

"It's so red!" said one.

"It's a bit of a dump," said another. "Too much lava for my taste."

As they followed the signs to the 'Headquarters' the route was eerily quiet. No more zombie pigmen came to attack them, no more minecarts full of TNT were sent their way.

"Be on edge," Dave told everyone, "we're probably walking into a trap."

Eventually the iron corridor ended, just as Porkins had said it would, and they found themselves walking across the Nether. In the distance they could see the cobblestone castle, but still they saw no pigmen or witches.

"Wait," said Carl, "can you hear that?"

Dave could just about make it out too. It sounded like a lot of people. A lot of people yelling and screaming.

They cautiously made their way forward. The voices got louder as they got nearer.

"I think those are villagers," said Sally.

As they got nearer Dave could hear that she was right. It sounded like hundreds of villagers, all yelling for help, but he couldn't see where the voices were coming from.

Then they came over a ridge, and Dave realized why he hadn't been able to see the villagers until then. A huge pit had been dug in the ground; its walls lined with iron blocks, and inside it were hundreds of villagers.

"Help!" they yelled, as Dave and the others cautiously looked over the edge, "let us out!"

It was hard to understand what the villagers were saying, with so many of them talking at once, but Dave eventually got the gist of it: they were the villagers from the other towns and villages who were going to revolt against Herobrine. Just like in Greenleaf, the zombie pigmen had launched a surprise attack in the night. They'd all been marched into the Nether and left in this pit.

"We have to get them out," said Sally.

Dave was scanning the rocky landscape for signs of zombie pigmen or witches.

They must be nearby, he thought. *They must know*

we're here.

Then he heard a voice from one of the rocky cliff tops
above them.

"Hello, Dave!" it said.

Dave looked up. One moment there was no-one there,
but then Dotty appeared. And then another witch, then
another, then another, until there were around twenty
witches, all looking down at them.

"So good to see you again, Dave," grinned Dotty.
"Potion of invisibility. You've got to love it."

Dave noticed she was standing next to some sort of
iron device. Then he noticed other iron devices, all
manned by witches.

"You recognize these, I'm sure," said Dotty, tapping
one of the iron devices. "A TNT cannon. I think some of
my sisters tried to blow you up with one before."

"We did," said another voice. It came from a tall witch,
who Dave vaguely recognized. "But he played a clever trick
on us, making the zombie piggies attack us. But that won't
be happening this time, because we have this."

The tall witch pulled out a golden staff with an
emerald on top.

"Trotter's staff!" gasped Porkins.

"It never really belonged to Trotter," said Dotty. "Lord
Herobrine just lent it to him, and that fat pig betrayed
Lord Herobrine's trust by being an idiot. Now Lady

Isabella has it, and we have complete control over all the pigmen."

"That's right," said the tall witch, Isabella.

"*Zombie* pigmen," said Porkins angrily.

Dotty laughed.

"Aww, are you offended, piggy?" she laughed. "What a precious little snowflake you are."

"Look," said Dave, "I'll hand myself over to Herobrine if you just let the villagers go. You still need them to work in your mines, don't you?"

"We did," said Isabella, "but now we have you, I think Lord Herobrine may have no use for them anymore. All he wants is to get the End. If you'd told him how to get there before, none of this would have happened."

"Besides," said Dotty, "Lord Herobrine has decided that villagers are too much trouble. So he's working on a new magic staff—one that will let him control *all* zombies. It's not quite ready yet, but he's decided that he wants to turn all of you into zombies anyway: so you're ready when the time comes."

There were terrified shouts and pleas from the villagers inside the pit, all of them begging to be let out, begging not to be turned into zombies.

"Right," said Isabella, "Dave, piggy, creeper, and all your friends, it's time to get in the pit. Either you get in of your own free will or we blow you to bits. There are five TNT cannons aimed at you; there's no escape."

Dave looked at Carl and Porkins, but they looked as clueless as he was. What were they going to do?

"Come on piggy," Dotty said, grinning down at Porkins. "Don't you want to join all your pigmen friends?"

Suddenly an arrow struck Dotty in the head. She toppled down from the cliff and landed with a *smack* next to the pit. Then *poof*, she was gone.

"*Zombie* pigmen," said a voice from above. "Those freaks aren't pigmen anymore. You witches need to know the difference."

Dave looked up and saw an army of pigmen—not zombie pigmen, but actual pigmen—standing on the cliffs above the witches. The one who'd spoke was a huge pigman with a barrel chest, holding a bow and arrow.

"You came!" Porkins said happily.

"We did," said Elder Crispy. "We came to fight."

CHAPTER FOURTEEN
Zombie Potion

"Get them!" Isabella screamed. "Kill them all!"

Porkins watched as a huge battle broke out on the cliffs above, between the pigmen and the witches. Suddenly zombie pigmen were appearing everywhere as well, coming out from wherever they'd been hiding.

Zombie pigmen charged at Porkins, Dave, Carl, Sally and the Greenleaf soldiers, who charged back at them. It was another chaotic battle, with swords clashing and arrows flying. At one point Porkins almost fell into the pit, but a pig-girl saved him, grabbing his hand just in time.

"Watch your step," she grinned at him.

"Thanks," said Porkins.

"Pat, watch out!" another pigman yelled. The pig-girl pushed Porkins out of the way just before a potion thrown by a witch could hit them. It shattered on the ground, the liquid inside it exploding into a blue fireball.

*

Carl was having the time of his life, battering zombie pigmen with his iron arms, sending them flying.

"Come on then!" he yelled. "I'll take you all on!"

A witch tried to throw a potion at him, but Carl quickly grabbed a zombie pigman and threw it at her.

"Who would have thought that fighting could be so much fun?" said Carl to himself.

He was just about to charge into another group of pigmen when he spotted some zombie pigmen in the distance carrying something along. It looked like a giant bucket, and he could make out a green liquid sloshing about inside it.

Oh no, thought Carl. *That's all we need.*

He knew what that green liquid was, he'd seen it once before, back in the Nether; it was the liquid that King Trotter had tried to use to turn them into zombies. It hadn't ended well for Trotter, he'd turned himself into a zombie instead.

The bucket was far too big for one zombie pigman to carry, so they were carrying it as a group, bringing it towards the pit.

So that was their plan, thought Carl. *They were going to get us all in that pit, then pour the liquid onto us, turning us all into zombies.*

Carl ran towards the bucket-carrying zombie pigmen as fast as his iron legs could carry him. He had almost reached them when something smashed into his chest, exploding in a burst of blue fire. He looked up and saw two witches above him with potion bottles. They threw bottle after bottle, sending him staggering backwards.

"Argh, stop!" yelled Carl. He stepped backwards and, to his horror, accidentally bashed into the giant bucket. It tipped over, the green liquid flowing down towards the pit.

"No!" Carl yelled.

*

Dave looked up when he heard Carl yell. The battle was raging all around him, but on the other side of the pit he could clearly see a green liquid flowing down a rocky slope towards the pit. Villagers, pigmen and witches alike were jumping out of the way of the liquid, but the villagers in the pit had nowhere to go.

That's the zombie-making liquid! Dave realized, to his horror.

Dave knew he could never get there in time, but he saw Porkins nearby, fighting back-to-back with a female pigman.

"Porkins!" Dave yelled. "Stop that liquid!"

*

Porkins turned and saw the green liquid.

"Cover me," he said to Pat the pig-girl. "Make sure to keep those zombie blighters away from me!"

Porkins took off his rucksack, reaching in and grabbing any blocks he could find. Then he quickly placed the blocks down—*thunk thunk thunk thunk thunk*—to block the pit.

SPLOSH! The liquid hit the wall and stopped, now just a big puddle of green on the ground. Porkins breathed a big sigh of relief, but then he felt something wet on his hand. He looked down and saw a drop of the green liquid had landed on his skin.

"Oh," he said.

*

The battle was practically over. The last of the witches were running away and there were very few zombie pigmen left. Dave breathed a sigh of relief, but then he looked over and saw Porkins on the ground, looking ill.

"What's wrong with him?" Dave said, rushing over.

Sally had Porkins's head resting on her lap. The female pigman was there too, as was Carl, leaning down in his iron golem suit.

"It's all my fault," said Carl. Dave had never heard the creeper sound so upset.

Then Dave saw what was wrong: an infection was creeping up Porkins's arm, the flesh turning green and rotten.

"He's turning into a... a zombie," said Sally, wiping tears from her eyes.

"No," said Dave. "No no!"

"Looks like... this is the end for me, old chap..." said Porkins weakly, giving Dave a smile. "But don't feel sad... I had a great adventure... with you and Carl... my two best friends."

"There must be something we can do!" said Dave. He was crying now too.

"You know... that there's no cure for zombie pigmen," said Porkins. "Just promise me that you'll continue your quest... find the ender dragon. Prove to the world that you're a... a hero."

Dave had never felt so helpless. He could see the zombie infection rising up Porkins's arm; it was almost at his shoulder now. Soon Porkins would be a zombie pigman, a mindless creature, all of his memories lost forever.

Dave pulled out his diamond sword.

"Get back," he said to Sally.

"Dave, what are you doing?" she said.

"Please, get back," said Dave.

Porkins's eyes were closed now. It wouldn't be long before the infection would spread to his brain, Dave knew. He'd seen the same happen to Trotter.

Sally placed Porkins's head down on the ground and then stood back.

"What are you doing?" said Carl to Dave.

"Saving our friend," said Dave. And he swung his sword down...

CHAPTER FIFTEEN
Goodbyes

Elder Crispy brought Isabella before Dave and threw her on the ground.

"My men Nathan and Ricco found this one trying to escape," he said gruffly. "And she had this on her." He pulled out the gold and emerald staff and threw it at Dave. Dave caught it.

"Thank you," Dave said. "What made you guys come and join us? Porkins said you refused to fight when he came to see you."

"We did," said Elder Crispy, "but something he said stuck with me. He said that if we don't stick together, people like Herobrine will keep on winning."

"Pah," said Isabella. "Lord Herobrine will get his revenge. You just wait and see."

Elder Crispy looked around.

"Where is Porkins? I want to thank him."

Dave sighed. "He..."

"Hello old bean!"

Porkins walked towards them, his torso wrapped in bandages.

"Do you really think you should be up and about?" said Dave. "You need rest."

"I can rest later," smiled Porkins.

"What happened to you?" Elder Crispy said, looking at Porkins's bandages.

"Oh this?" said Porkins. "Dave cut my arm off."

"He what?!" snarled Crispy, drawing his bow.

"No, no, it's a good thing!" laughed Porkins. "If he hadn't cut off the infection, I would have turned into one of those zombie chaps. He saved me."

"I must say," said Carl, coming over to them in his iron suit, "you look awfully happy for someone who's just lost an arm."

"Well, I guess there's no arm in that," said Porkins. And then he started laughing hysterically.

"Carl," said Dave, "I think that potion Sally gave him to stop the pain has made him go a bit light-headed. Do you mind carrying him?"

For once the creeper didn't complain, and he reached down and picked Porkins up in his arms. Dave could see from the look on Carl's face that he still felt guilty.

They built a staircase down to the pit so the villagers

could get out. There was much hugging and laughter and promises from the different settlements to help each other if there were any more attacks in the future. Carl, Porkins and some of the injured villagers from Greenleaf made their way back home, and the other villagers began making their way back to their settlements as well.

Next Dave threw the gold staff in the lava. For a moment it just sunk down, and then they was a KRAKOOM and it exploded.

"You know, Herobrine could just build another one," said Elder Crispy.

"I know," said Dave. "But from what that witch was saying, they seem to be quite hard to make. We might slow him down a bit at least."

Dave had been worried that Herobrine might appear during the battle, but he never had. Dave suspected that Herobrine knew that his invasion was finished, so hadn't bothered to get involved. Dave led a group of villagers and pigmen down the iron corridors, following the signs that led to 'Herobrine'. He knew in his heart that Herobrine would probably be long gone, but they needed to check.

Eventually they reached a nether portal with the word 'Herobrine' above it. Dave stepped through first, and found himself in the bedrock castle, where Herobrine had kept him, Porkins and Carl prisoner. It was empty now, but Dave and the others searched the castle anyway. There was nothing there; all of Herobrine's things had been removed.

Afterwards, everyone said their goodbyes, ready to go back to their own homes.

"Make sure you keep in touch," Sally said to Elder Crispy. "We all need to stick together. Herobrine is still out there somewhere."

"Aye," said Elder Crispy. "You too."

Dave went back with Sally and the remaining Greenleaf villagers, taking Isabella with them as a prisoner. When they got there, Carl had tucked Porkins up in bed in Sally's house. Porkins was fast asleep.

"Will he be alright?" Carl asked Sally.

"He'll be fine," said Sally. "He's healing well. I... I'm sorry again about Adam."

"That's not your fault," said Dave. "You fought well. Everyone in Greenleaf did. You should all be proud."

Sally smiled, then went off to her bedroom and left Dave, Carl and Porkins alone.

"It's my fault anyway," said Carl miserably. "I messed up."

"No you didn't," said Dave. "And anyway, Porkins is going to be fine."

Suddenly there was a flash of purple light and a villager appeared in the room next to them, his face hidden in shadow.

"No he's not," said the villager in a gruff voice. "None of you are, unless you do exactly as I say."

Dave stood up and drew his sword.

"Who are you?" he demanded.

The villager stepped forward into the light. His face was scarred and he had an eyepatch on one eye, but Dave knew that face.

"I'm you, Dave," the villager said. "I'm you from the future."

"Oh dear," said Carl. "Something tells me that things are about to get awfully complicated..."

TO BE CONTINUED...

EPILOGUE

Adam was colder than he'd ever been. Until last week he'd never even left Greenleaf, and now he was wandering through a snow biome, exiled from the place he called home.

This is all Dave's fault, he thought bitterly. *If it weren't for him, I'd still be at home, and I'd still be with my wife!*

Suddenly he tripped over in the snow. He tried to push himself to his feet but he was too weak.

Maybe I'll just stay here, he thought miserably. *What's the point in going on?*

"Get up, Adam."

Adam looked up. Standing over him was a man in blue jeans and a t-shirt. The snowstorm was so thick that he couldn't see his face.

"Who... are you?" said Adam.

"Do you hate Dave with all your heart?" said the man.

"Do you want to get vengeance on him and revenge for all the wrongs that he has done to you?"

"Yes!" said Adam. "Yes, more than anything!"

"Then take my hand," said the man, reaching down. "And join me."

Adam reached up and took Herobrine's hand.

Made in the USA
Columbia, SC
10 December 2020

27204402R00062